'What's all the talk about dust?' Roger said, flashing his lights and half-blinding poor Ted's only eye. 'We all know it's dusty! We all know we have been left up here and...' he stopped to frown at Ted, who was feeling for the edge of the chest and pulling himself out and onto the floor '...we all know we are never getting out of here.'

Prince Regal is trying to keep everyone's spirits up while Roger the tipper truck seems completely determined to upset everyone... The problem is that the toys have been in Bobby's parents' attic for a very long time. Even Merrybelle is beginning to think that they really might have been forgotten...

First published in Great Britain in 2015 by Jennie Orbell
Cover Design & Illustration © Gaile Griffin Peers 2015

Paperback Edition
ISBN 978-1517520571

FIRST PAPERBACK EDITION

9 8 7 3 6 4 5 0 1 2

https://jennieorbell.wordpress.com

Prince Regal
and the
Forgotten Friends

by
Jennie Orbell

Illustrated by Gaile Griffin Peers

It was dark and dusty in the old blue chest
Where Merrybelle lived with all the rest
Of things once loved, but now without use
All alone, under the dark high roof.

Chapter One

Merrybelle yawned and stretched out her dusty wings one after the other.

'Watch out Merrybelle!' Prince Regal, the rocking horse, said from high above the toy chest, 'you nearly poked old Ted in the eye …his only eye, I might add.'

Ted also yawned and rubbed hard at his left eye. 'Morning,' he said, in that deep teddy-bear voice. 'It's alright Merrybelle, you didn't hurt me.'

'Thank goodness for that,' Merrybelle said, stroking Ted's faded brown head. 'This box seems to get more crowded every day.'

'Nowhere to stretch out your wings, is there old thing?' Prince Regal said. 'I've told you before, come and sleep on my back. It's wide and long, plenty of room for a small fairy.'

Merrybelle sneezed.

'You shouldn't stroke my head, you know I'm full of dust …we are all full of dust,' Ted said, still rubbing at his left eye. He hadn't been quite the same since he'd lost his right eye over by the window. It had fallen out, without warning, and rolled between the floorboards and no amount of tweaking and fiddling from his friends could reach the eye from the narrow crack. It stared sadly back at them from the darkness beneath the floor. Poor Ted without an eye. And the poor eye without Ted.

'What's all the noise, can't anyone get a lie-in around here,' Roger, the tipper truck, grumbled, pushing his way from the bottom of the chest and reaching the top with one of his wheels spinning.

'What's all the talk about dust?' Roger said, flashing his lights and half-blinding poor Ted's only eye. 'We all know it's dusty! We all know we have been left up here and…' he stopped to frown at Ted, who was feeling for the edge of the chest and pulling himself out and onto the floor '…we all know we are never getting out of here.'

Prince Regal rocked a bit and bent lower until his nose was next to Roger's window. 'Listen, Roger,' Prince Regal said in a low, gruff voice, 'don't keep going on and on about it, there's a good chap. Some of these toys believe that one day that door over there…' he nodded towards the attic door '…one day that door will open and we will be taken from this dusty place and have lives to live again. You, saying that we are never going to leave here, just makes everyone sad.'

Roger didn't answer. The silly horse was wrong.

No one was going anywhere. They had all been put in the attic when the people in the house no longer wanted them …when Bobby no longer wanted them.

He dipped his lights and said nothing. They would see. They would all see. No one was coming – ever.

It wasn't the worst place for a toy to be
And they had each other for company
And Minton the mouse kept them up to date
With the things that went on beyond the gate

Chapter Two

Shortly after nine Minton arrived, squeezing his fat brown body through the hole in the roof, scurrying across the floor. As he scurried he squeaked.

'Listen! Listen! I have news!'

Ted and Merrybelle looked down at him from the back of Prince Regal, where they rocked back and forth …back and forth.

'It won't be anything exciting,' Roger shouted above the sound of Prince Regal's rocking, 'it never is. Just squeaks and nonsense about life beyond this place. We are NEVER going to have a life beyond this place. How many more times do you silly toys need telling? I say stuff Ted in that hole in the roof and keep the silly squeaky mouse thing out!'

'We will do no such thing,' Prince Regal neighed, making all the toys jump.

Little Wilhelmina-plastic-robin fell off the edge of the box where she'd been standing, singing her high notes. Robins liked to do that kind of thing.

'Everyone here has a voice and everyone here shall be heard,' Prince Regal said.

His voice was calmer now and, as he stopped rocking, Ted slipped down from the horse's high back and Merrybelle spread her wings and fluttered down to stand besides Ted.

'What is it, Minton, what news do you have?' Merrybelle said excitedly.

'He doesn't have ANY news. None that's worth listening too at any rate,' Roger said. 'And who wants to hear the voice of a silly mouse that only last week got himself stuck in a baked bean tin. I ask you, what kind of silly mouse does that?'

'It wasn't my fault,' Minton squeaked. 'It was slimy and beany inside and I couldn't get out without slipping.'

'Then you shouldn't have gone in it in the first place, should you?' Roger said, and flashed his lights. Ted fell over. Minton scurried over to Ted squeaking in alarm.

'You need to get your other eye from under the floor boards, Ted, and then you won't keep falling over. I think you need both eyes.'

'Like we haven't tried,' Roger said with a grin on his face. 'That eye is staying under the floor boards. Stuff the bear in the hole that's what I say. Let's make some use of him.'

'Shame on you, Roger,' Merrybelle said, helping Ted to his feet and flying around him, dusting him off.

'We will manage to get Ted's eye one day. Until then we toys will help him.'

'Oh right, will we indeed Mrs Fairy – who is still in love with Bobby. He isn't coming back for you, you know.

You will never sit on the top of another Christmas tree, not ever. Bobby has gone, gone, gone.'

With those cruel words, that hurt Merrybelle more than anyone could ever know, Roger honked his horn and drove himself off to the far end of the attic.

Prince Regal watched him go. Something had to be done about that truck. It made everyone sad. Yes, it was true, Bobby wasn't coming back.

The little boy who had loved all the toys and each Christmas trimmed the tree before placing Merrybelle on the top, on the highest branch, had grown up. He'd become a man and moved away. No one was coming. Roger was right. But there was a way of saying these things and Roger's way was wrong.

'Well …well …this is it,' squeaked Minton. 'Are you ready for this news?'

Merrybelle flapped her wings and nodded. Ted rubbed at his eye and nodded. Wilhelmina jumped into the air and flew an excited circle and the other toys rushed up to form a line, all ready for the news from Minton the mouse. Prince Regal took a deep, deep breath and hoped that for once Minton did have something good to tell them.

It wasn't that hard for a mouse to read
The letters were big and easy indeed
They said that the house
was up for sale
Interesting news
– and quite a tale

Chapter Three

The toys looked from one to the other. Merrybelle stopped flapping her silver wings and folded them carefully.

Ted stopped rubbing at his eye and blinked. Wilhelmina robin messed-up her landing and ended up upside down in Prince Regal's long mane. Prince Regal snorted.

What did it all mean?

'So …so …go on then, tell me that isn't exciting news?' Minton squeaked in his high-pitched voice, while standing on his two back legs and cleaning a cobweb from his whiskers. 'Exciting or what?'

'But what does it mean,' Merrybelle whispered.

Her eyes were wide, slightly excited, slightly frightened. 'What does it mean?'

'Mean? What does it mean?' Roger shouted, racing across the floor from where he'd been sulking in the corner.

'It means we are all going to be left here forever and ever. No one is coming now. No one knows we are here.'

Prince Regal snorted angrily. 'If that is all you can keep saying, Roger, I suggest you go back to sulking in your corner. You are frightening the younger toys.'

Roger flashed his lights angrily. 'I'm telling you …if the people downstairs have gone away no one knows we are here and no one will come. Bobby went away and he has never come back for us.'

Larry, the yellow giraffe, started to cry. 'Hush, hush now. It's alright. We have lived here for a long time now, we can live here for a bit longer,' Merrybelle said kindly, fluttering up onto his back and folding a wing around his long neck, giving him a gentle squeeze.

'Exactly!' Roger spat. 'Exactly. We will all live here forever …just like I've always said.'

'Just because this house is being sold, what makes you think Bobby's mother and father have already gone away?' Prince Regal said with a great deal of horse sense.

'Ah, yes,' squeaked Minton, 'I forgot to tell you that bit.'

'Well go on then!' Roger roared. 'Tell us the whole sad thing before I drive over there and squash you.'

Minton shook a little and allowed Ted to pick him up before he continued.

'I heard the lady next door saying that Bobby's mother and father have gone to live in a place where they will be looked after because they are old and can't look after themselves any longer, and that they will have lots of nice things to eat and that they will be happy there.'

'Well I'm glad someone's happy,' Roger snapped.

Larry Giraffe started to cry again.

Prince Regal began to rock, so fast that the floor boards shook and Roger almost turned upside down.

Wilhelmina took off, frightened, and perched up high in the roof, well out of the way.

The other toys jumped back into the blue chest.

'We will NOT be forgotten,' Prince Regal neighed loudly.   'Do you hear me, all you toys?

Do *YOU* hear me Roger?

We will *NOT* be forgotten.

New people will come and they will find us. We will all be found.'

Roger slammed his tipper back shut and shouted, 'Yes, we will be found …and then we will ALL be thrown away.'

Merrybelle dreamed of Christmases Past
When Bobby had lifted her gently, like glass
Placing her carefully high on the tree
Where Merrybelle watched the whole family

Chapter Four

Merrybelle wiped away a silent tear.

Sniffles and gentle sobs could be heard from each shadowy corner of the attic and from deep inside the chest.

Only Roger remained tearless.

Roger, who had been the cause of all the tears.

Merrybelle wasn't a silly Christmas fairy, she knew that no one was coming. She knew that they would all have to stay in the attic, unloved, unused and uncared for. It had been that way since Bobby grew up and moved away.

Merrybelle had loved Bobby.

She still loved Bobby. She had loved the way his hair stuck up at the front and no amount of brushing would ever get it to lie flat. She loved his bright blue eyes. She had watched him from her high place on the Christmas tree.

Watched him getting warm in front of the fire, eating his tea, playing with Jitter, his naughty cat.

Jitter often used to climb the tree and sit at the top with Merrybelle and Bobby had climbed onto the arm of the chair and reached up and removed Jitter, leaving Merrybelle sitting proudly on the top.

Toys didn't really get old …not like children.

Toys got a bit scuffed, a bit tatty and some, like Ted, lost a few bits here and there. But toys really stayed the same.

Little boys and girls didn't. They grew up and became mummies and daddies and they had no need for toys. Merrybelle wiped away another tear and sniffed. She had cried so much that her wings were wet and she couldn't fly up onto Prince Regal's back when he called her and asked her to do so.

Instead, he bent his proud white and brown spotted head and whispered against her ear.

'Don't cry Merrybelle. It will all be alright.'

Ted walked up looking damp and a big soggy.

'Yes, don't cry Merrybelle, Regal is right – it will all be alright.'

Merrybelle smiled. Prince Regal and Ted were her best friends.

They wouldn't tell her a lie. But, she knew that they were just trying to be kind to make her feel better and that secretly they probably didn't think that anyone was coming either.

In time the sniffles began to dry
Only so many tears a toy could cry
And things returned to how they had been
Until Minton rushed in to tell what he'd seen

Chapter Five

'…And this is the truth?' Prince Regal asked. 'You heard these words with your own ears?'

'Yes, yes, I did,' squeaked Minton.

'But what does it mean?' Ted said, rubbing at the place where his missing eye should be.

It was troubling him a lot lately and all the rubbing was wearing away his fur.

'It means that one of those big truck things is coming to take away all the furniture,' Minton squeaked, stopping to look at Roger who was motoring across the floorboards towards them. 'And I mean a proper truck thing,' added Minton very bravely, 'not like Roger with a tipper thing that pops up and down all on its own.'

Roger flashed a headlight. He'd been struggling lately to make his left headlight work.

'What do you mean by that, mouse? There's nothing wrong with my tipper. I'll have you know that Bobby used to fill me full of stones and pull me along on a piece of string. I never once tipped over or lost a single stone. MY tipper is perfect.'

Prince Regal took a deep breath and rolled his eyes. He was a patient horse, but Roger and his upsetting ways were really beginning to make him cross.

Regal didn't want to lose his temper because he was old and wise and knew that nothing was ever gained by losing your temper.

He had to remind himself of this very often. 'I think what Minton means is it's a truck without a tipper back. Is that right, Minton?'

Minton shrugged.

He didn't mind one little bit if Roger thought he was saying his tipper wasn't perfect.

Roger was a bully and Minton still hadn't forgiven him for running over his tail a week ago and then pretending that he hadn't seen Minton sitting there cleaning his whiskers. And besides, he could be very brave indeed when Prince Regal was around.

'So …a truck is coming to take away the furniture?' Ted repeated.

'Yes!' Minton said.

'And you know this because?' Prince Regal said.

'Because he's had his brown little nose stuck into someone else's business …as usual,' Roger said, 'and I don't care one way or the other. It doesn't change a thing. We aren't furniture. We won't be taken.'

With that Roger drove off and parked beneath a dusty, old chair.

Merrybelle and Wilhelmina robin flew down from the roof and settled on Prince Regal's back.

Wilhelmina messed-up her landing again and ended up in Prince Regal's tail.

'Did I hear right? Minton, did you say that people are coming?' Merrybelle said excitedly. 'Coming for us?'

Minton raised himself up onto his back legs and twitched his whiskers.

He no longer looked excited …but a little sad.

'I'm not sure if they are coming for you, Merrybelle …or you, Prince Regal …or you, Ted and Wilhelmina, …or any of you, I just heard from that lady next door that someone is coming to take all the furniture away.'

From the dark corner, beneath the dusty chair, a headlight flashed.

What excitement
noise from below!

HOUSE
2 HOUSE

Doors opening and closing,
voices speaking low

Furniture being lifted and taken away

The toys held their breath
— and started to pray

Chapter Six

'Can you hear them? Can you hear them?'

Wilhelmina robin twittered, flapping madly and circling the attic ten times.

'They are here! They are coming. Any minute now. Any minute now. Oh I feel sick.'

Wilhelmina crash-landed into Ted who, sadly, didn't see her coming because of his missing right eye.

They fell over together laughing and rolling across the dusty floor.

'Shush!' Prince Regal said. 'You know the rules, you two, NO movement when there are people about.'

Ted got to his feet and Wilhelmina took off for another few circuits before repeating her crash landing, this time knocking over Larry Giraffe.

Prince Regal shook his mane and snorted.

'Wilhelmina! Go and perch somewhere and be quiet!'

The little bird obeyed and fluttered up to perch on Prince Regal's head.

'Sorry,' she said, hopping up and down and tickling his head with her nails, 'but it's SO exciting, I can barely keep my wings still. Any minute now and the attic door will open and we will all be saved. Saved …saved …saved.'

Ted and Merrybelle joined Wilhelmina on Prince Regal's back and quietly, very quietly, he began to rock …and they all waited.

****

Sometime later Minton squeezed through the hole in the roof and scurried across the floor, squeaking as he scuttled. 'They've gone …they've gone… they have ALL gone. There's nothing at all left in the house. I climbed up onto the window ledge and looked in the window. There's nothing left …nothing at all.'

'Except US!'

The voice boomed from under the chair.

Roger motored over with both headlights flashing on full-beam and his horn blasting.

The toys all covered their ears against the terrible sound. 'I TOLD you! I told you!'

Roger shouted, blasting and blasting his horn. 'I TOLD you no one would come but you wouldn't believe me, would you? You silly, silly toys!'

The hours passed slowly and still no one came
And even Prince Regal could hardly explain
Could Roger be right and here they would stay?
For ever ...and ever ...and ever a day.

Chapter Seven

The attic was filled with sounds of whispers. Toys huddled together in little groups.

Wilhelmina fluttered and crashed between the groups of friends listening, here and there, to what they were saying before reporting back to Prince Regal, Merrybelle and Ted.

Larry Giraffe and his little group of King the lion,

Bertha the elephant and Spike the rhinoceros were saying that they had always hoped that they would get out of the attic one day but now it seemed that Roger, the bossy tipper truck, had been right all along.

Oscar, the tatty blue rabbit and his little group of Digger the mole, Flitter the hare and Mac the pink squirrel were whispering so quietly that Wilhelmina couldn't catch a single word.

Roger had no reason to whisper and was stating very loudly, even loud enough for him to be heard outside on the street, that he'd been right all along.

Cecil the cement mixer turned his drum a few times in agreement but the others, Red the bus, and Basil the train, said very little.

Prince Regal was, in their opinion, wise and sensible, and he hardly ever shouted …except at Roger and that was only because Roger kept upsetting everyone and making everyone cry.

By night time everyone had left their little groups and gone to bed in the big blue chest, where they all tried to accept that no one was coming.

Merrybelle sat for a while on the edge of the chest, resting beneath Prince Regal's chin.

She had been a lucky Christmas fairy.

She knew that some fairies only got lifted out of their boxes at Christmas time and then put away in the dark until the next year but Merrybelle had never been put away, not until Bobby grew up and moved away.

Bobby had taken Merrybelle from the tree after Christmas and placed her lovingly on the top of the bookshelf. It had been a bit dusty up there but not as dusty as the attic and Merrybelle had watched Bobby all year round.

She gave a sigh and slipping into the chest, folded her delicate wings and closed her eyes.

If she couldn't be with Bobby she could close her eyes, sleep, and dream about him.

Minton hurried and scurried – but no
Before he could tell them, a noise from below
A creak, a groan, and the attic door rose
A head appeared, followed by a nose

Chapter Eight

There came the sound of gentle creaking followed by the sound of loud creaking. A narrow beam of light ran across the attic beams followed by a wide beam of light as the attic door opened. Prince Regal stopped rocking at once.

Roger was parked on the top of the attic door testing his wheels and as it lifted it sent him racing across the floor and crashing into the dark corner where he tipped over and ended up on his back.

Wilhelmina robin flew into Prince Regal's tail and hid there, shaking like a jelly. Merrybelle, Ted, Flitter the hare, and Oscar, the tatty blue rabbit, leapt into the blue chest as fast as they could. Flitter grabbed Digger the mole as he leapt and they all ended up in a heap.

'What is it? What is it?' Ted whispered into Merrybelle's ear as he peered towards the light. 'What's happening?'

'Shush, Ted,' Merrybelle whispered back, 'I need to see.' She clutched tightly onto the edge of the chest as Flitter and the others buried themselves deeper into the dark, safe chest. 'It's …a …man.'

'A man?' said Ted, rubbing his eye. 'A man?'

Merrybelle watched as the man pulled himself up into the attic, placing his hands on the dusty floor before rising up. He scratched his head and ran a hand through his hair. He looked confused.

Behind him another human appeared. A small human. A boy. Merrybelle's eyes were as wide as saucers. Her little fairy heart was beating fast. The small human looked like Bobby. But that couldn't be right, could it? That couldn't be right at all.

'Well, Josh, look at this lot. Thank goodness I remembered to look in here.'

'What are they, Daddy?' Josh said. The man walked over to Prince Regal and gently touched his head.

Then he plucked Wilhelmina robin from the rocking horse's mane and looked at her.

'What are all these toys, Daddy?' Josh repeated.

The man wiped his eye with a finger. 'These were my toys, Josh, when I was your age. Look …this is Prince Regal, my rocking horse. Prince and I had lovely adventures. We rode in The Grand National and with the American Indians. We had adventure after adventure.'

'But why are they here, Daddy?'

'Because …I grew out of them, Josh.'

Merrybelle stared at Ted. Ted stared back with his one eye. Together, in hushed voices they said, 'It's Bobby!'

Can it be real?
Can it be true?

Chapter Nine

The little boy wandered across to the blue chest.

'Daddy! Daddy! Look. A bear with one eye …and a Christmas fairy!'

Bobby gave Prince Regal another stroke before walking across to the chest.

He picked up Ted in one hand and Merrybelle in the other.

'Merrybelle!' Bobby said. 'So this is where Mother and Father put you.'

He turned Merrybelle round and round, smoothing her crumpled dress and gently stroking her wings.

'And Ted! What on earth has happened to you, my friend? Where's your other eye?'

Ted would have blinked if it had been allowed but Ted knew the rules – no movement of any kind when people were present. He wanted to look at Merrybelle because he knew she was smiling …but then Merrybelle was always smiling, she had simply been made that way.

'Can I have the fairy, please, Daddy?

Can we take her home and put her on our Christmas tree?

...And can we take this bear – even though he does have only one eye?

...And Prince – can we take Prince, please? Then I can have adventures too.'

Bobby's eyes looked very wet and he rubbed them with a finger.

'Of course, Josh. We can take Merrybelle and Prince and Wilhelmina ...and Ted – in fact, we can take them all. Look, here's Digger Mole and Flitter ...and more.'

Josh bounced up and down clapping his hands. 'Yes, Daddy, and they can play with my toys and they can all be friends.'

Bobby stroked Josh's head lovingly. 'Of course.'

Minton watched from the hole in the wall
As the toys were taken down to the hall
Nothing remained but darkness and dust
And a sad little truck - now left to rust

Chapter Ten

The toys waited in the hall – all arranged in the big blue chest. Every toy was going. Every toy was going to be loved and played with again.

Every toy, that is, except one.

Roger wasn't with them.

When the attic door had opened, Roger had been parked on it testing his wheels.

He'd rolled off the door and into the dark corner of the attic and no one could see him there.

Ted had a quick look to make sure that Bobby and Josh weren't anywhere close before shouting to Prince Regal.

'Roger's missing!

He rolled into the dark corner and no one could see him. What are we going to do? Poor Roger.'

Prince Regal twitched an eye. 'Shush Ted! No talking!'

'But what about Roger?' Ted said again. 'I know he was pretty horrible to me but it was only because he was scared. He really thought that we would never get out of that place. He wasn't really bad and Josh would love playing with him. Roger was great at carrying stones and sand and things. I don't want Roger to be left behind.'

'I don't want him to be left behind either,' Merrybelle said. Her throat hurt and she thought she might cry.

'Me neither,' said Flitter and Digger.

'And nor do I,' Prince Regal said, 'but I fear that there is little we can do to change it now.'

****

In the attic, Minton scurried and squeaked. 'For goodness sake …for goodness sake …move your wheels …flash your lights, Roger. No one knows you are here. You'll be left behind for ever if you don't hurry.'

Roger couldn't even be bothered to turn on his lights. He was forgotten …again. He had been right all along. He really never was going to get out of this place.

'Roger! Roger! Listen to me,' Minton squeaked. 'You are on your back …that's a good thing. I can climb on you and if I try really hard, and if you try really hard, I can tip you over.'

Roger shrugged as best a tipper truck can shrug. 'What's the point in that?'

Minton climbed up on top of Roger, dangling his tail in Roger's face. 'Because …if I can turn you over before they close the door the people will hear and come back to check. Now do as I say and try to turn over.'

'It won't work! I'm here to stay,' Roger said, shrugging again.

'I've never known such a sad toy in my whole life,' Minton squeaked. 'You have to be the saddest toy in the whole world. Don't you want to carry stones and sand and play with Josh in the garden? Don't you want to have your headlights cleaned and your tipper polished? What is wrong with you?'

'The other toys hate me,' Roger said.

Three tears slid across his upside down windscreen and rolled onto the floor.

He felt so sad that he couldn't even get his windscreen wipers to work to wash away the tears.

'Is THAT all?' Minton said with a squeaky giggle. 'They don't hate you. They just want you to be happy.'

'I would be happy if I could carry stones and sand again …and if that little person I saw earlier wanted to play with me,' Roger said with a sniff and two more tears.

'Then do as I say,' Minton squeaked crossly. 'And don't roll on me and squash me!'

Together they wriggled.

…And pushed.

…And heaved.

And then, suddenly, with a loud bump Roger was the right way up.

'Now what?' Roger said, panting a bit.

'Shush!' Minton squeaked, panting much harder than Roger. 'Listen! Someone's coming.'

Bobby's head appeared through the attic door. His face had a frown on it until he saw Minton sitting in the corner of the attic in front of Roger.

Then he grinned. 'Aah, it's a wee mouse making all that noise. Hi little fellow. And what's that you have there? It looks very much like Roger … It is Roger. How on earth did I miss you my old friend?'

Minton scurried off to the hole in the roof and watched as Bobby picked up Roger, lovingly dusting him off and wiping his headlights with the cuff of his jumper.

'Josh is going to love playing with you my old friend, just like I did,' Bobby said, before turning to take a last look around the attic.

Nothing remained. Nothing....

....Except....

What was that glistening and shining beneath the floor boards?

Bobby reached down and after a bit of a struggle closed his fingers around the shiny object and lifted it out.

He opened his hand and looked at the eye and Ted's eye looked back.

Minton jumped up and down, up and down, and simply couldn't stop.

It was going to be alright.

ALL the toys were going home

even Ted's eye.

Made in the USA
Charleston, SC
14 October 2015